P9-BZR-976

The Play

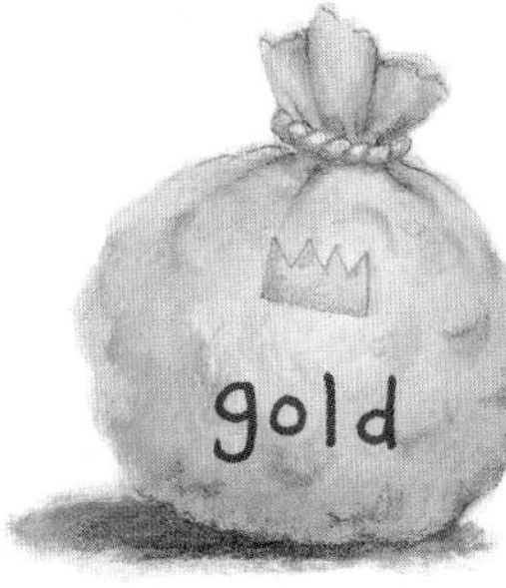

Monica Hughes

Illustrated by
Lindsey Gardiner

Rigby

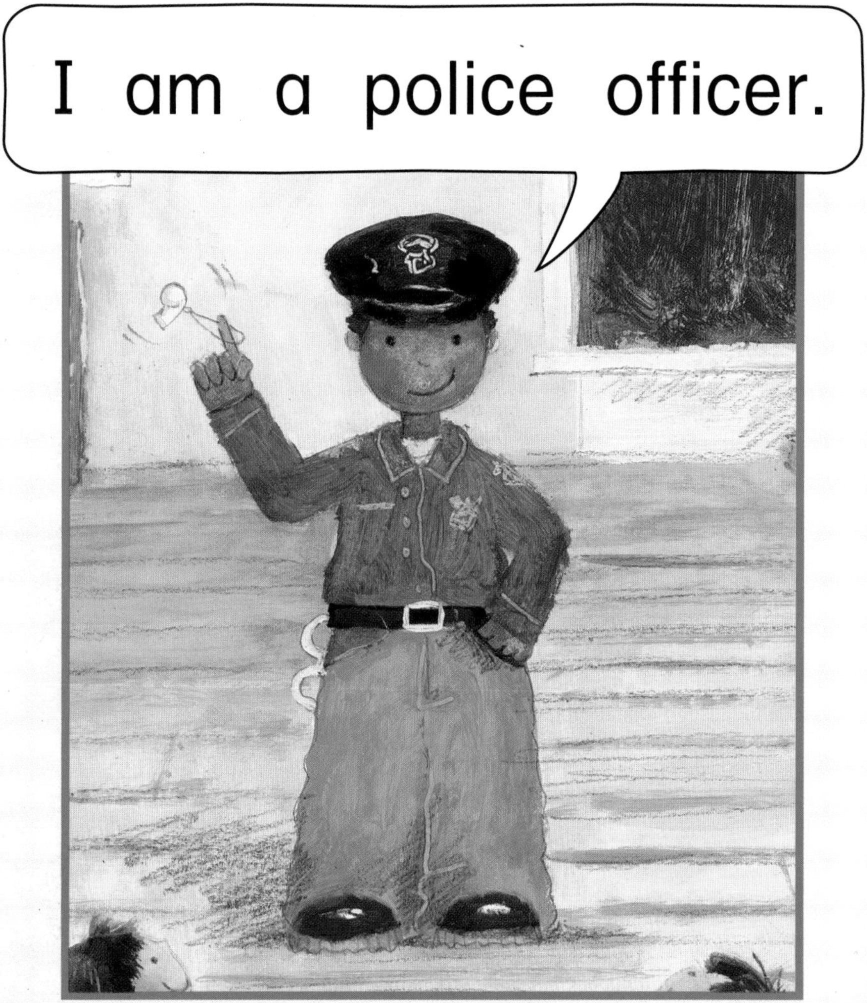
I am a police officer.

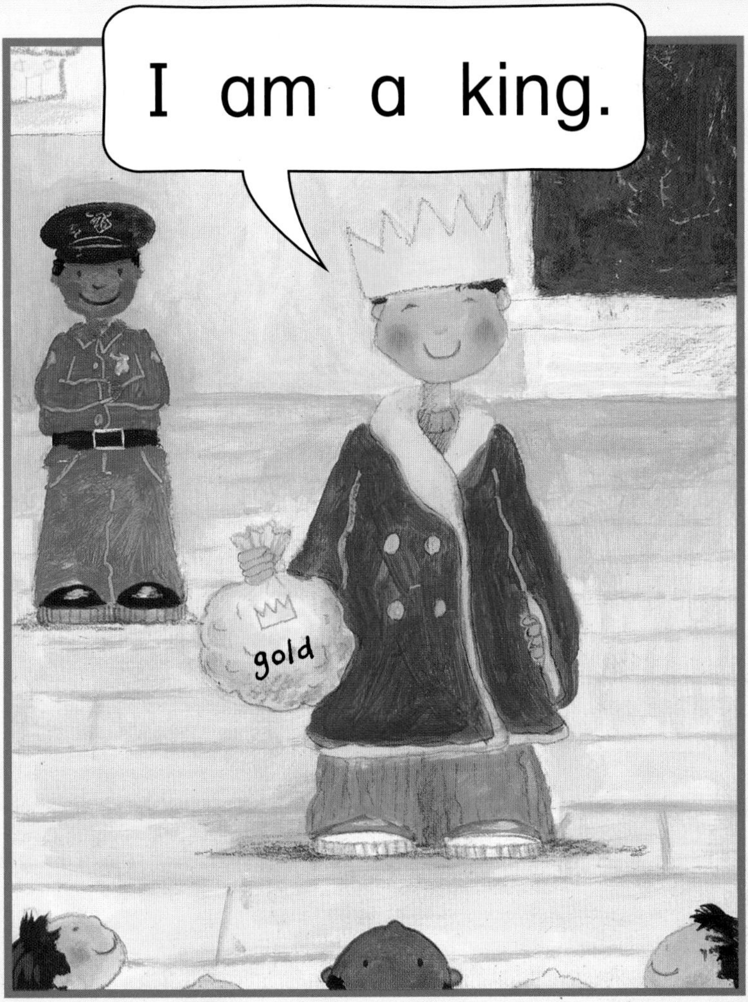
I am a king.
gold

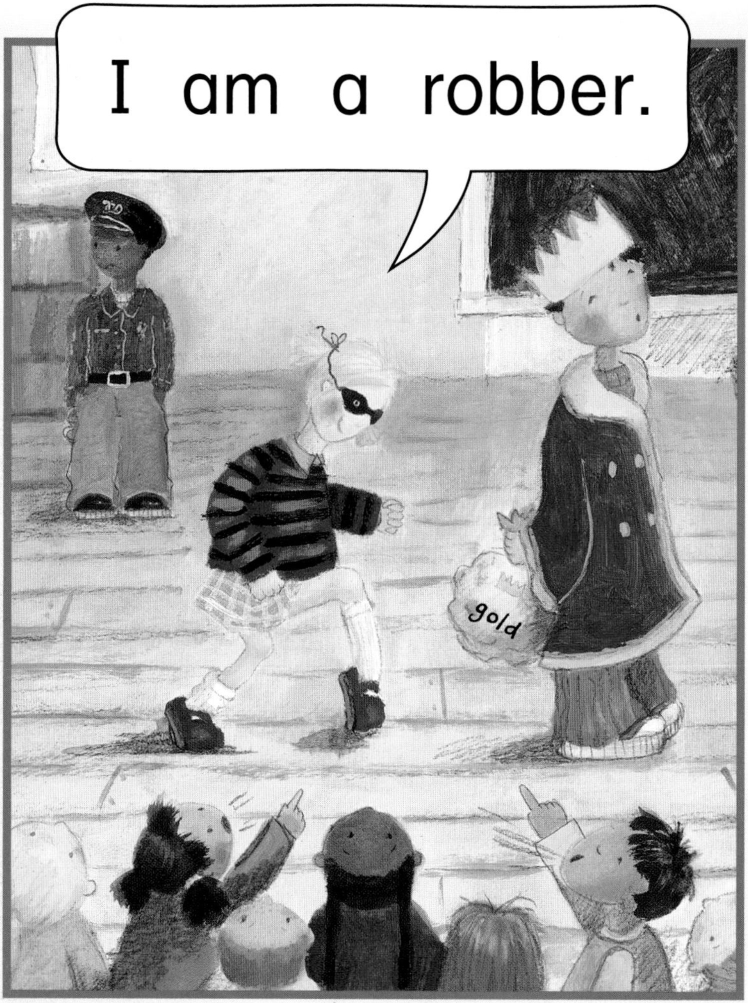
I am a robber.
gold

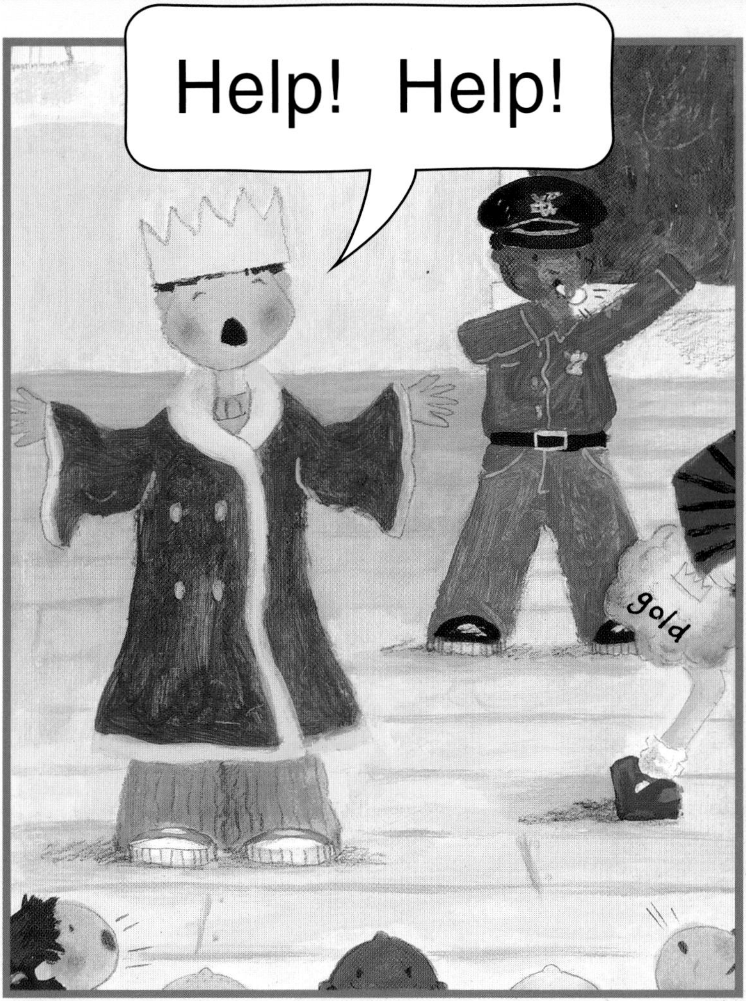
Help! Help!
gold

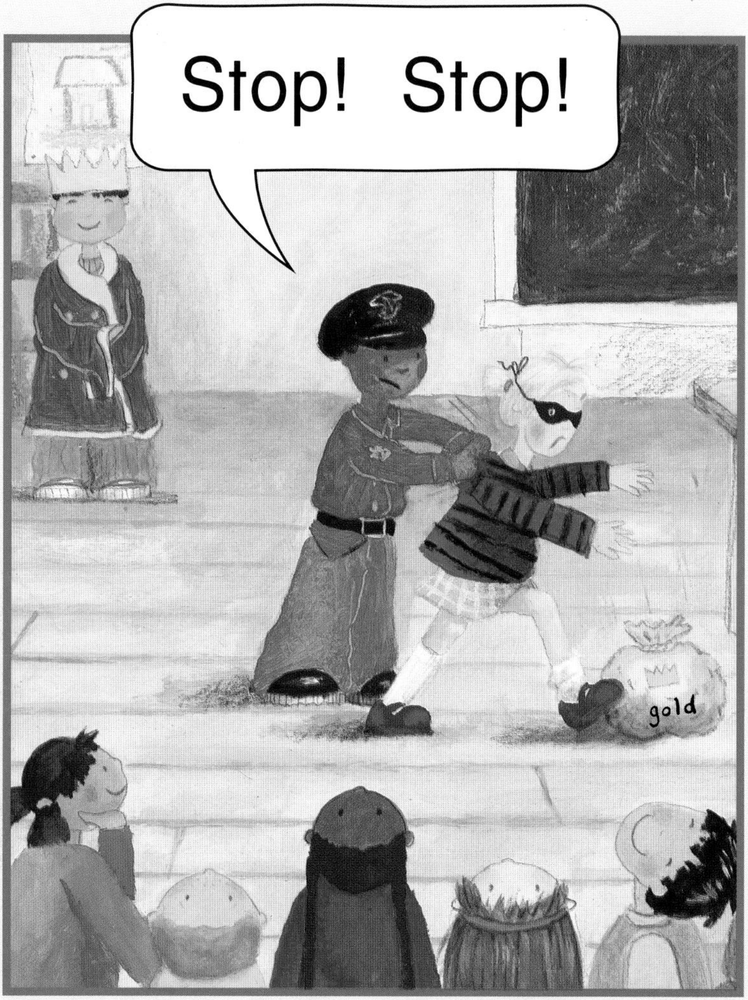
Stop! Stop!
gold

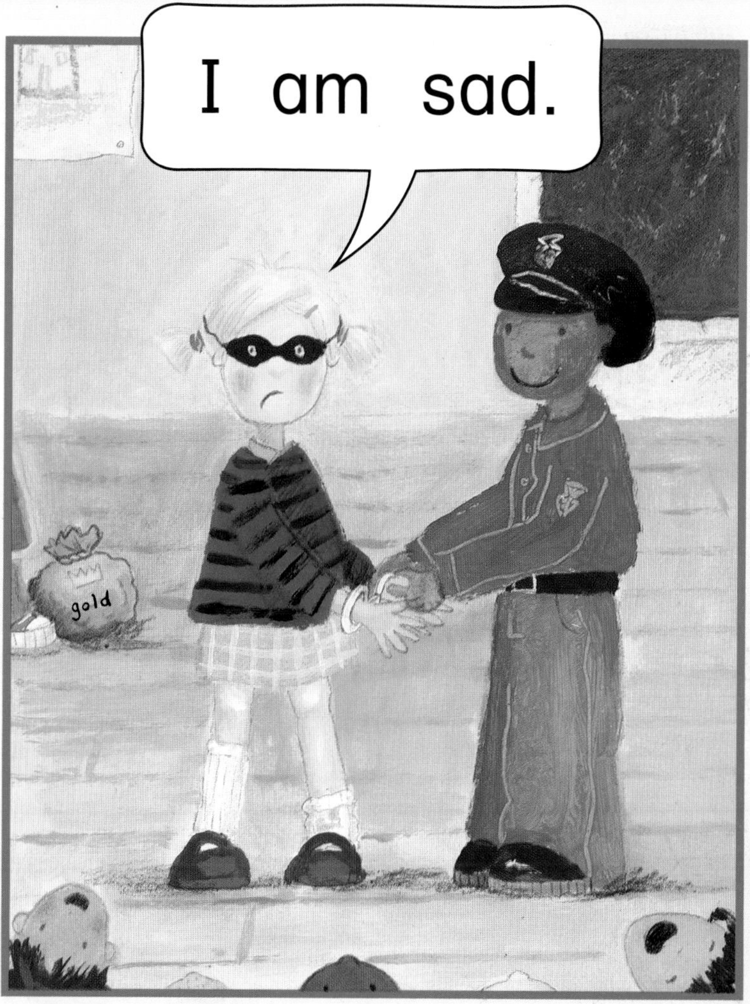
I am sad.
gold

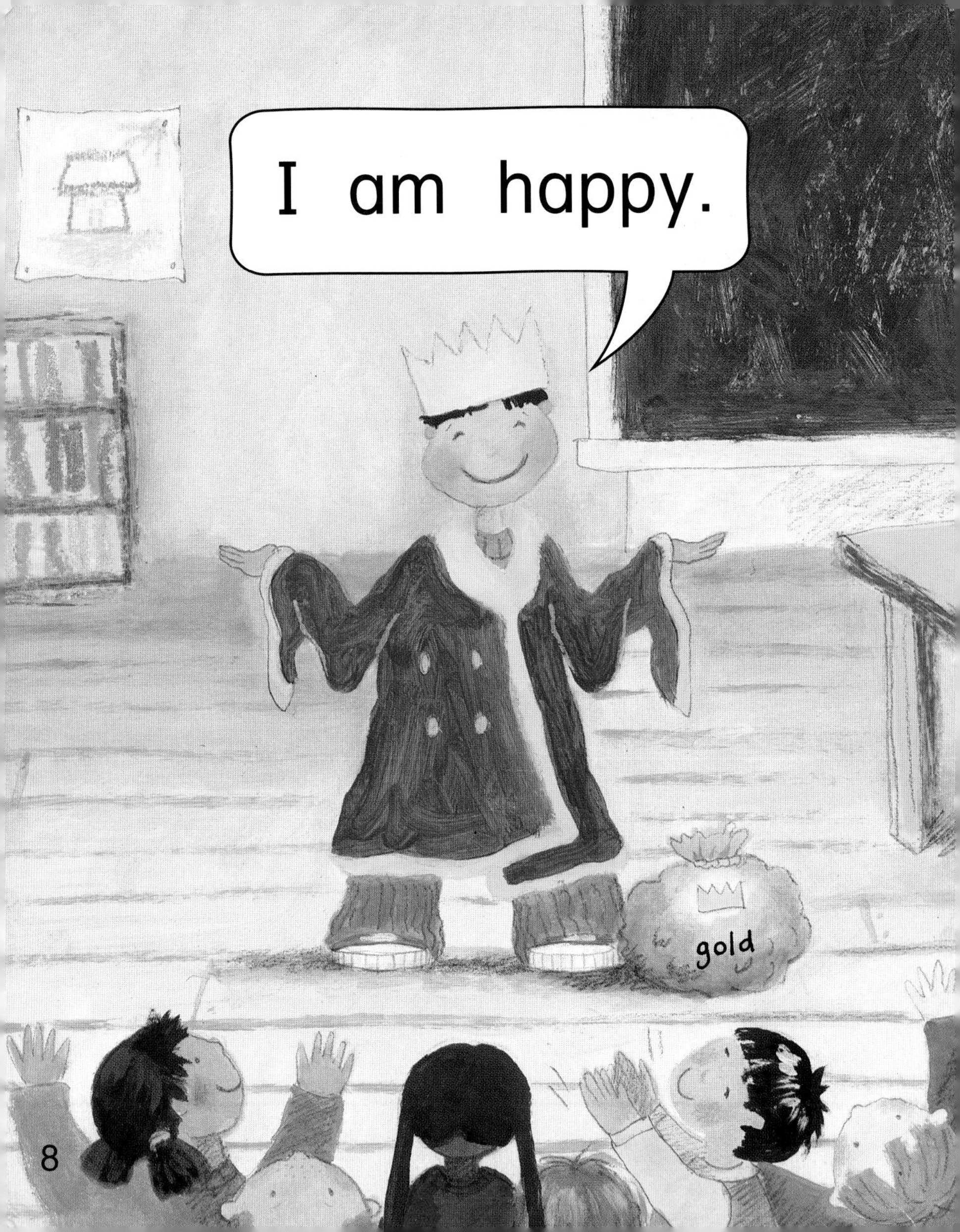
I am happy.
gold